THE JAR OF HAPPINESS

AILSA BURROWS

Once there was a little girl called Meg,
who invented her own kind of happiness.

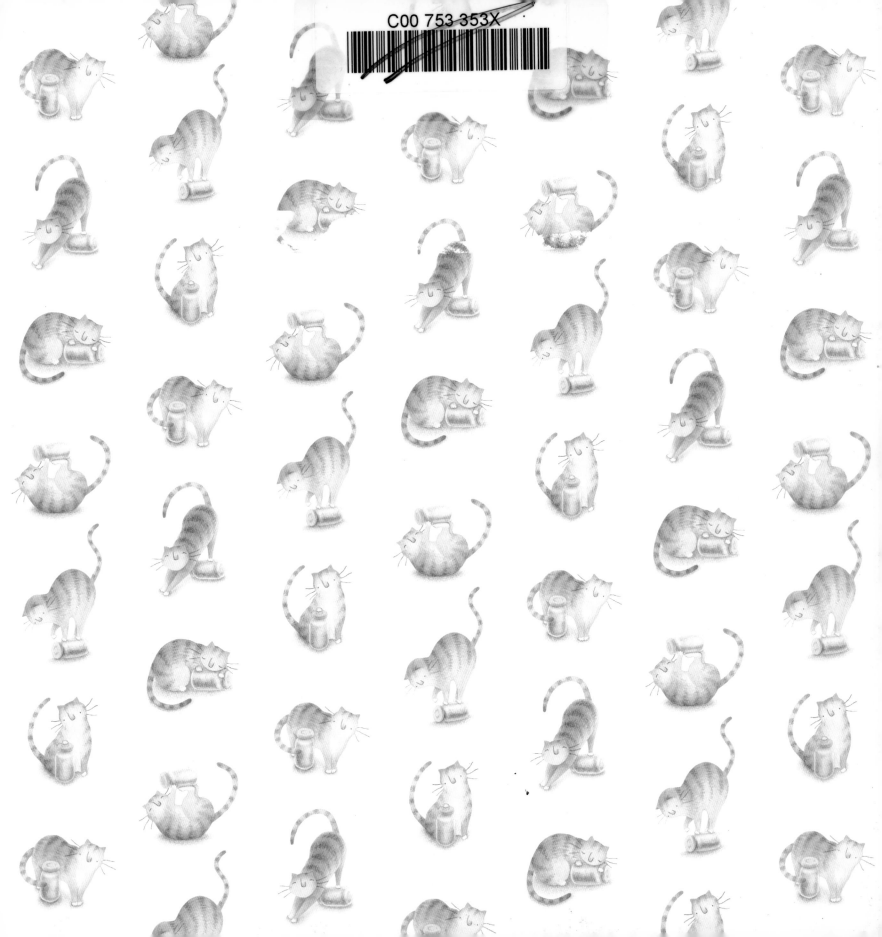

To Gareth, Fran, Timo, Flint and my parents

First published in 2015 by Child's Play (International) Ltd
Ashworth Road, Bridgemead, Swindon SN5 7YD, UK

Published in USA by Child's Play Inc
250 Minot Avenue, Auburn, Mainé 04210

Distributed in Australia by Child's Play Australia Pty Ltd
Unit 10/20 Narabang Way, Belrose, Sydney, NSW 2085

Text and illustrations copyright ©2015 Ailsa Burrows
The moral right of the author/illustrator has been asserted

ISBN 978-1-84643-728-1
CLP090215CPL07157281

Printed in Shenzhen, China

1 3 5 7 9 10 8 6 4 2

A catalogue record of this book
is available from the British Library

www.childs-play.com

It tasted of chocolate ice cream,
apple juice and sunshine.

And it smelled of warm
biscuits and the seaside.

It was red, yellow
and all of the other
best colours.

Meg took it everywhere with her.

She took it to her friend
Zoe, who was feeling
a little glum.

It cheered up Oma,
who felt a bit poorly.

Meg shared it with Leon too...

...though only when
he was being nice to her.

One morning
Meg could not
find her jar
of happiness.

She looked...

and looked...

...and looked and looked.

But she couldn't find
the jar anywhere!

Where could it be?

Meg visited Zoe, who showed her
how to make happiness out of smiles.

She visited Oma,
who gave her a bit of happiness
made from hugs and tickles.

And Leon explained how thinking
happy thoughts can scare away gloomy
feelings, bad smells and even monsters.

By the end of the day,
Meg still hadn't found her jar...

...but she had found plenty of happiness.

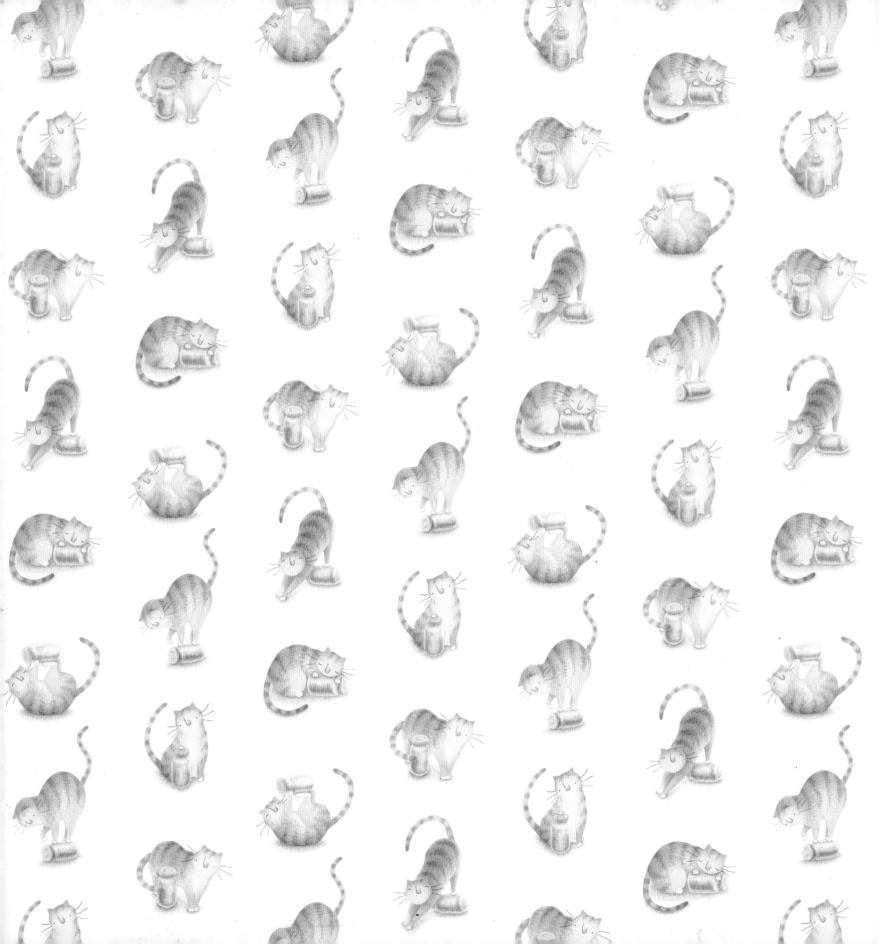